the most relaxing classical music ever

for solo piano

Chester Music

London / New York / Paris / Sydney / Copenhagen / Berlin / Madrid / Tokyo

Order No. CH 64053
International Standard Book Number: 0.8256.3393.1

Exclusive Distributors:
Music Sales Corporation
257 Park Avenue South, New York, NY 10010 USA
Music Sales Limited
8/9 Frith Street, London W1D 3JB England
Music Sales Pty. Limited
120 Rothschild Street, Rosebery, Sydney, NSW 2018, Australia

Printed in the United States of America

adagio for strings

By Samuel Barber

5

7

all love can be

(from *a beautiful mind*)

Music by James Horner
Words by Will Jennings

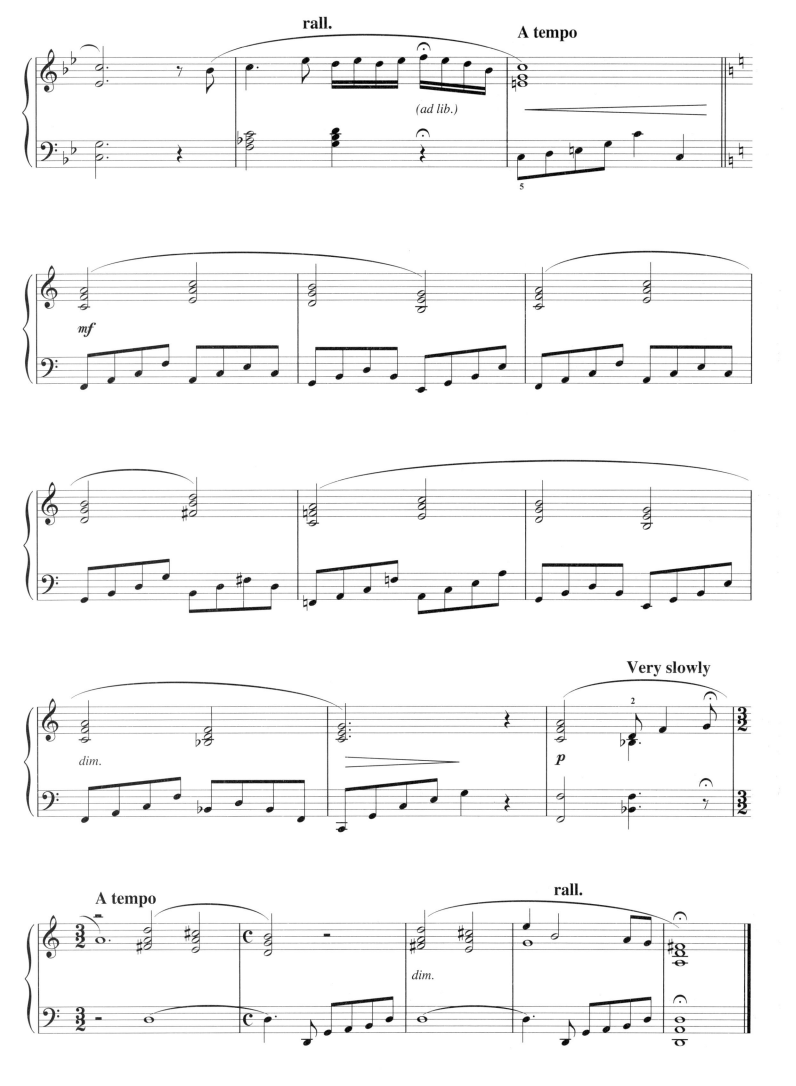

11

adagio of spartacus and phrygia

(from *spartacus*)

By Aram Khachaturian

accel. poco a poco

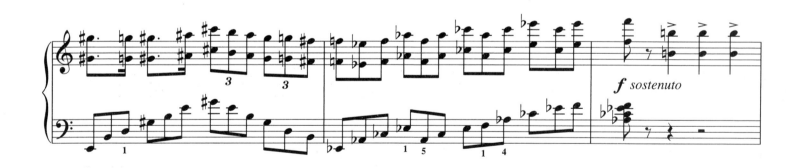

rall. **a tempo**

molto rit.

Lento

allegretto
from symphony no. 7 in A major (2nd movement)

By Ludwig van Beethoven

Allegretto (♩ = 76)

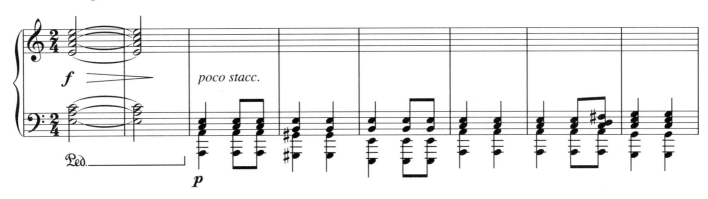

aria
from "goldberg variations"

By Johann Sebastian Bach

any other name
(from *american beauty*)

By Thomas Newman

Moderately

(con Ped.)

23

aquarium
from the carnival of the animals

By Camille Saint-Saëns

clair de lune
from suite bergamasque

By Claude Debussy

Andante espressivo

con pedale

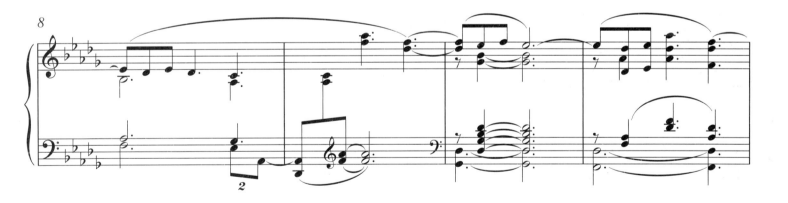

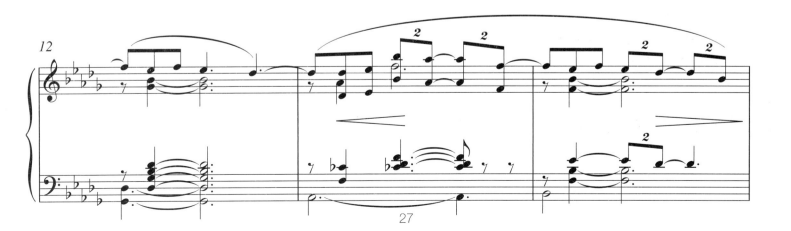

Tempo rubato

the ashokan farewell

(from the tv series *the civil war*)

By Jay Ungar

Freely, with expression

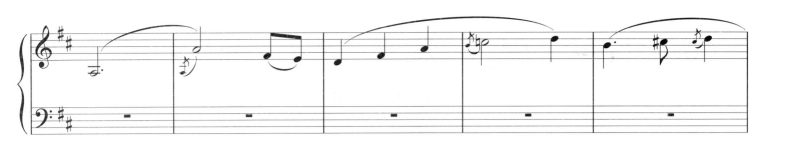

a tempo (but still a little freely) ♩ = *c*.88

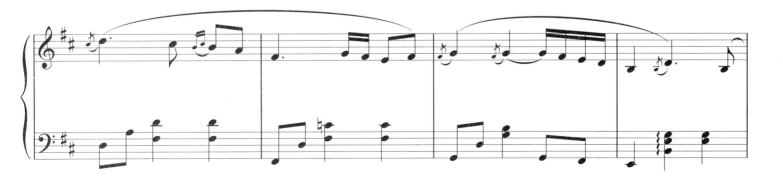

31

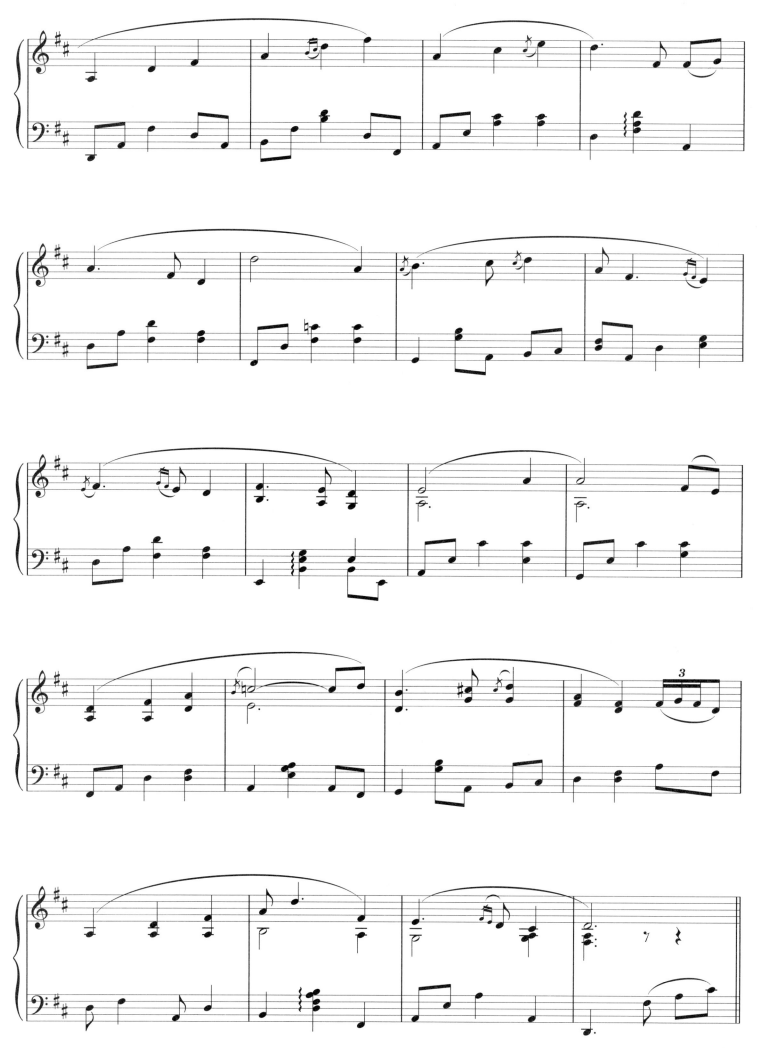

molto rit.

a tempo

poco dim.

rall.

autumn

from the four seasons (adagio molto)

By Antonio Vivaldi

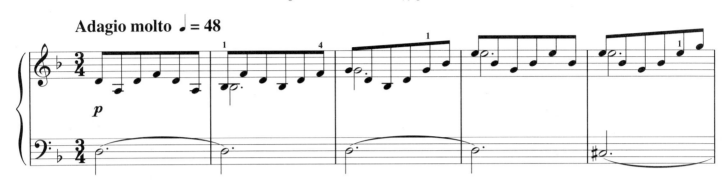

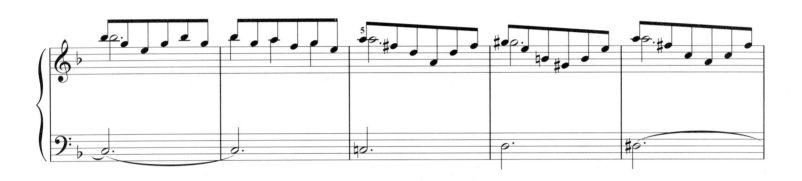

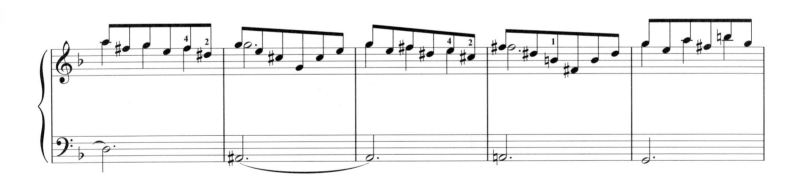

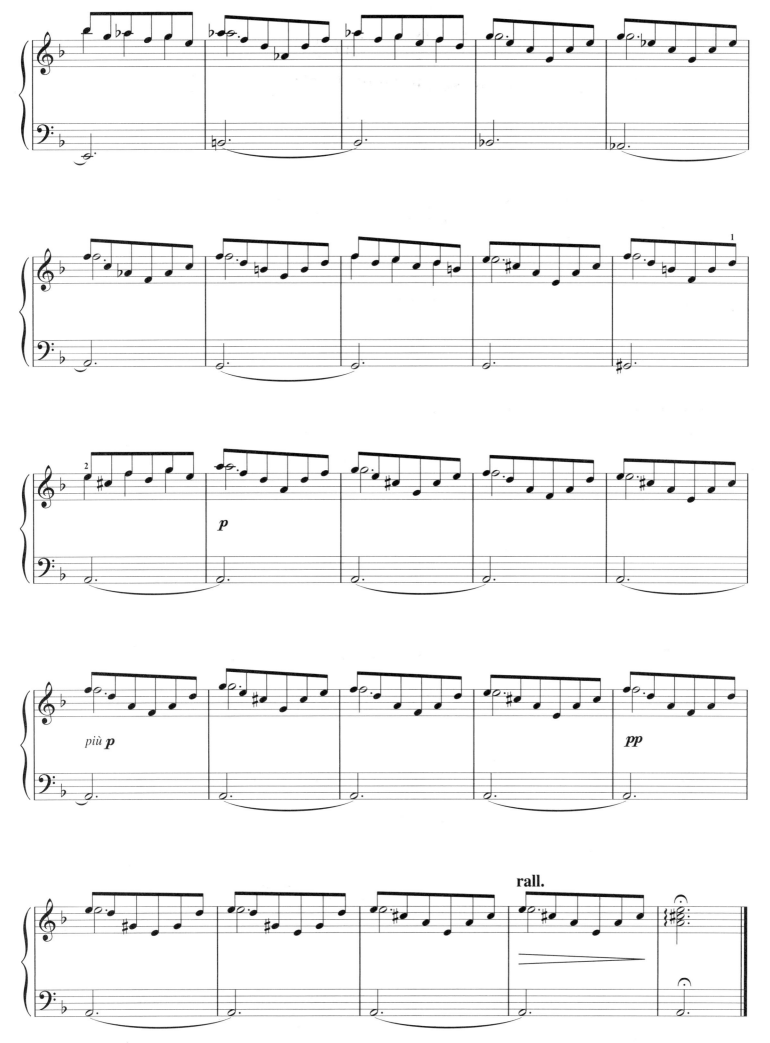

ave verum corpus
in D major, K618

By Wolfgang Amadeus Mozart

Slow

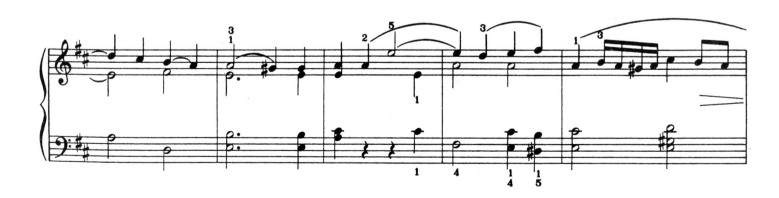

barcarolle
from the tales of hoffmann

By Jacques Offenbach

sempre più dolce   morendo

ppp

una corda

41

dance of the hours
from *la gioconda*

By Amilcare Ponchielli

Moderato ($\quarternote$ = c.160)
'THE HOURS OF DAY'

poco rit.   a tempo

Meno mosso ($\quad$ = c.132)
'THE HOURS OF NIGHT'
espress.

rit.   **a tempo**

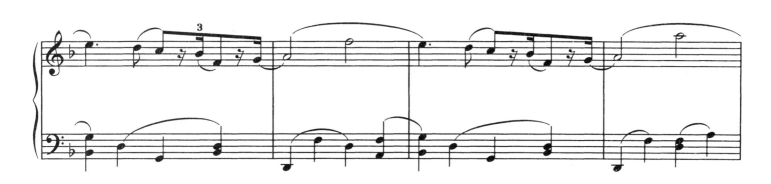

Allegro con brio (♪ = c.168)
'DANCE OF ALL THE HOURS'

l'amour est un oiseau rebelle

(habañera)

from *carmen*

By Georges Bizet

Allegretto, quasi andantino ♩ = 72

flower duet
from *lakmé*

By Leo Delibes

poco rit.

a tempo

rit. al fine

molto ten.

49

gnossienne no.1

By Erik Satie

Du bout de la pensée

Postulez en vous-même

Pas à Pas

Sur la langue

51

gymnopédie no.1

By Erik Satie

Lent et douloureux

lacrymosa
from requiem

By Wolfgang Amadeus Mozart

the lamb

By John Tavener

With extreme tenderness - flexible ♩ = c. 40

[moving forward]

Poco meno mosso

A tempo - moving forward

Poco meno mosso

lara's theme
(from *dr. zhivago*)

Music by Maurice Jarre

Moderately ♩. = 60

largo
from symphony no.9 ("from the new world")

By Antonin Dvořák

Largo (♩ = 48)

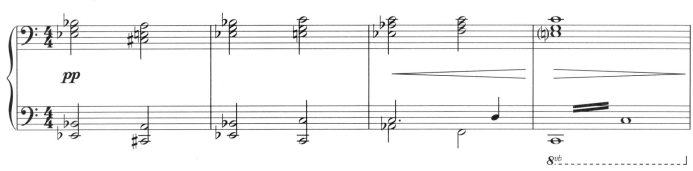

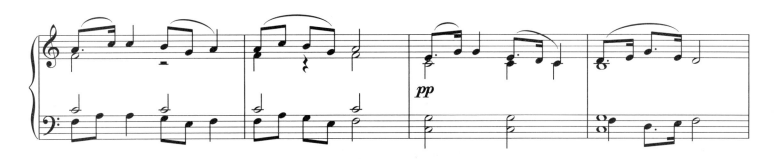

liebestraum

By Franz Liszt

Poco allegro, con affetto ♩. = 54

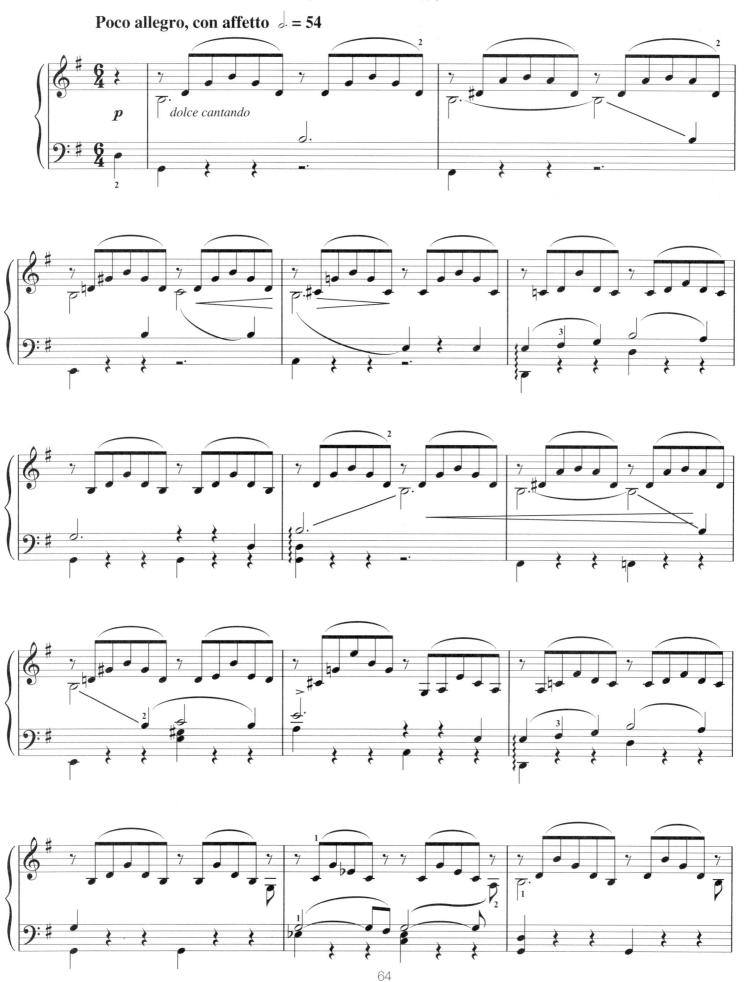

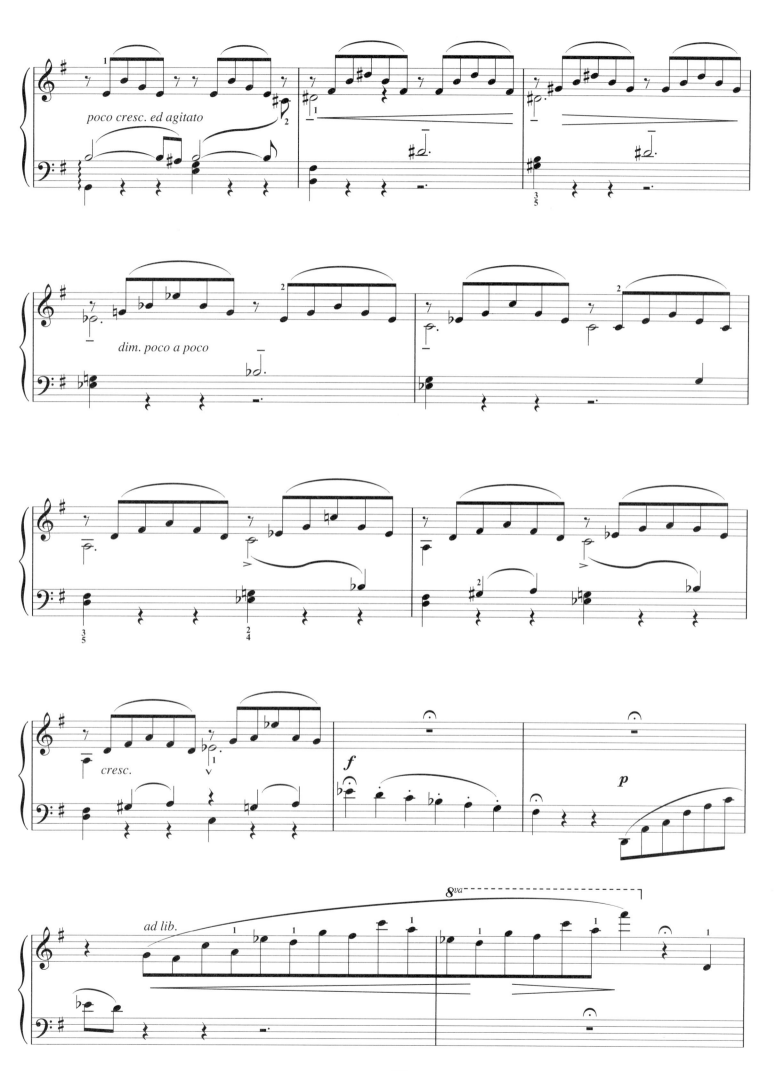

Tempo primo

poco a poco ritenuto

love theme from *romeo & juliet*

By Nino Rota

Slow and expressive

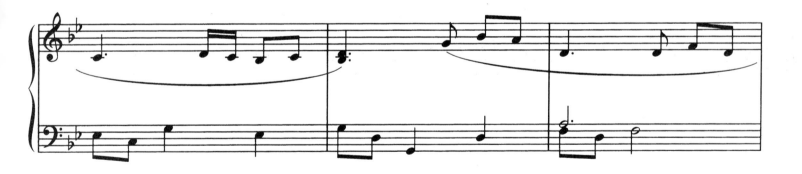

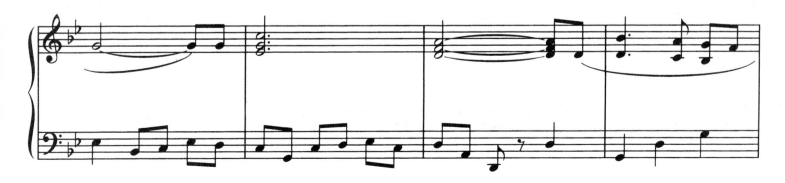

nessun dorma

from *turandot*

By Giacomo Puccini

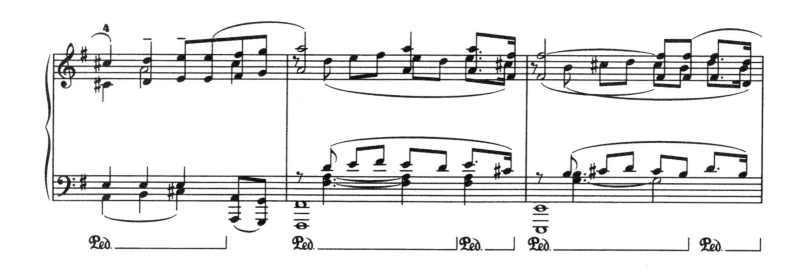

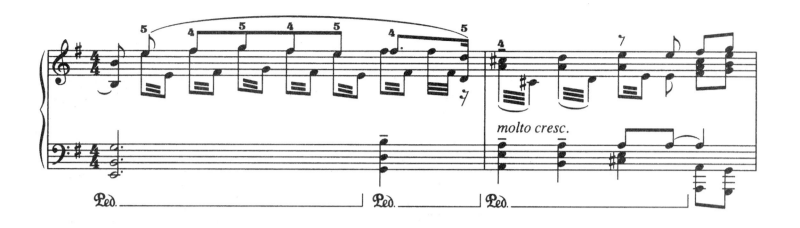

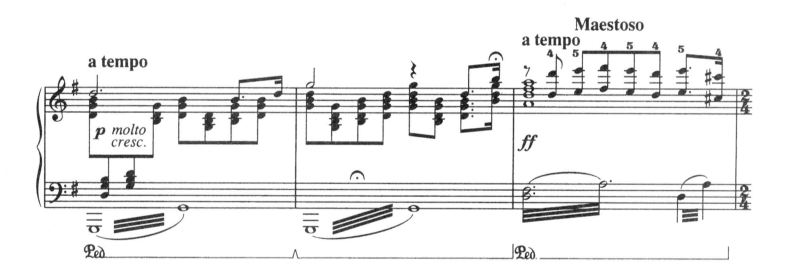

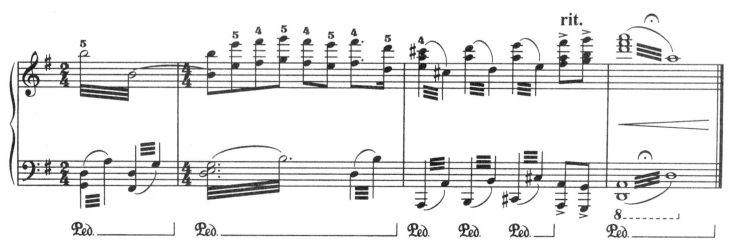

'moonlight' sonata op.27 no. 2
(adagio sostenuto)

By Ludwig van Beethoven

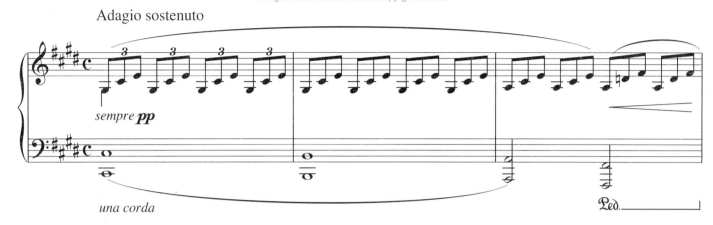

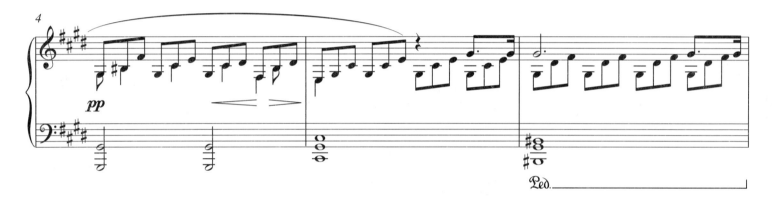

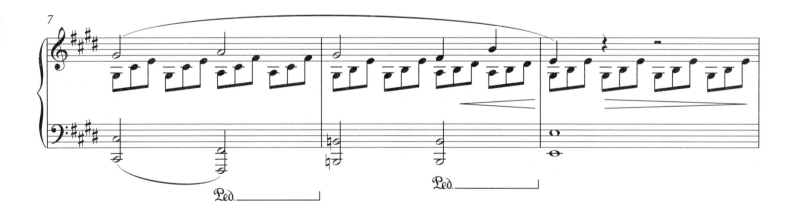

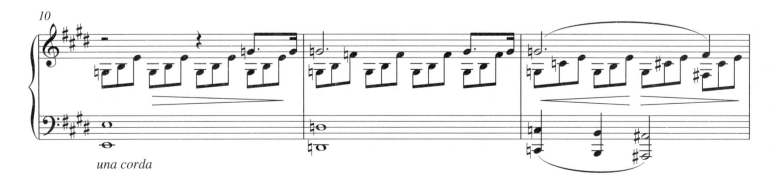

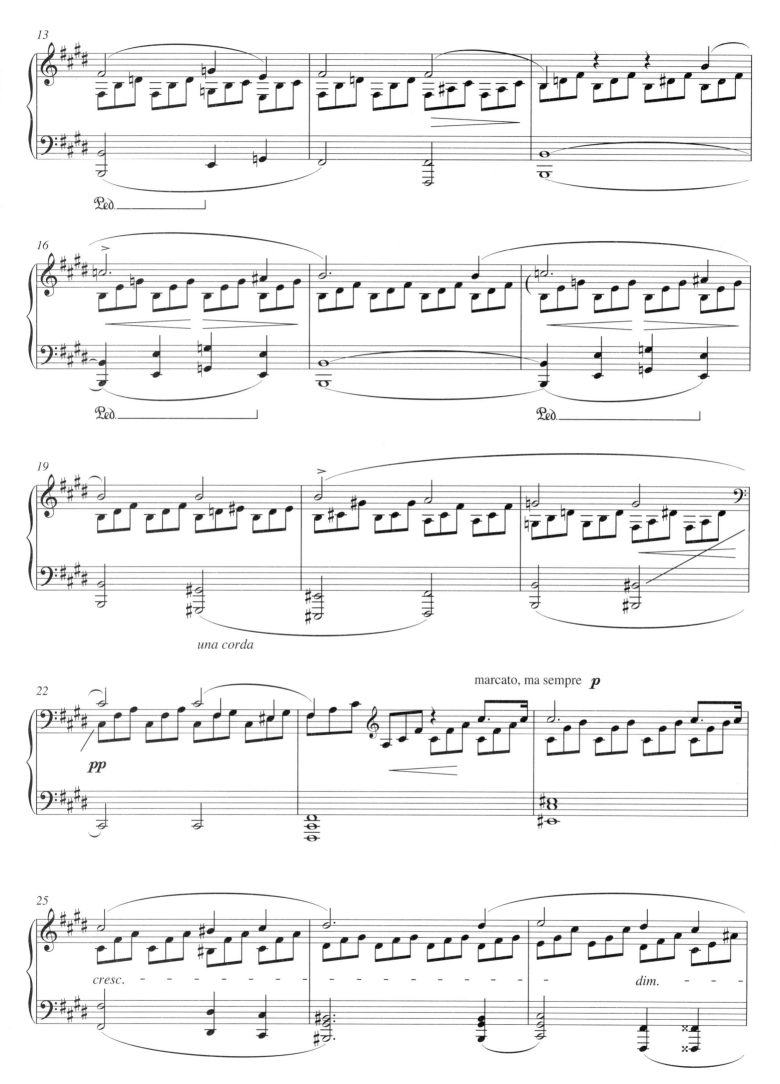

una corda

il basso sempre

poco rit.

a tempo

più marcato del principio

una corda

grave

76

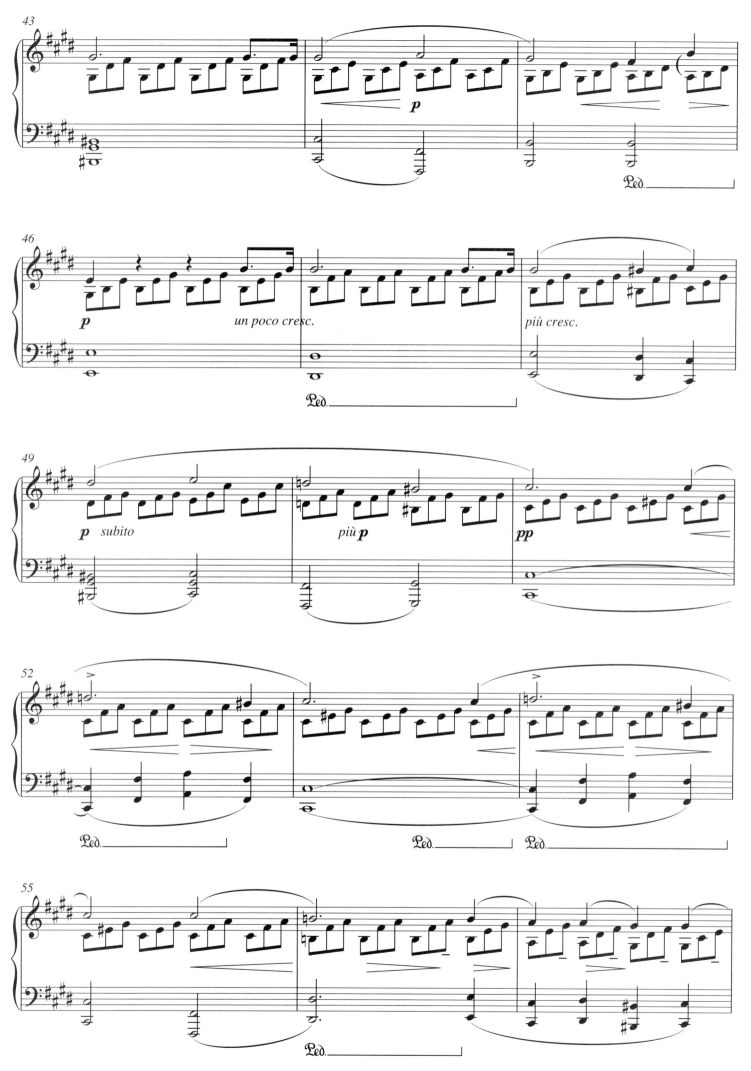

theme
from *midnight cowboy*

By John Barry

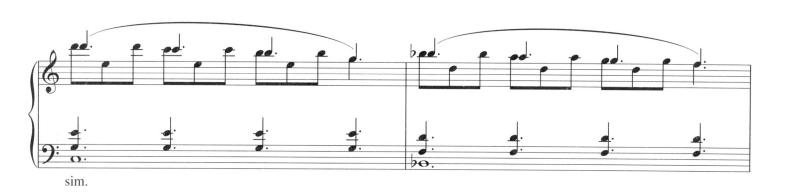

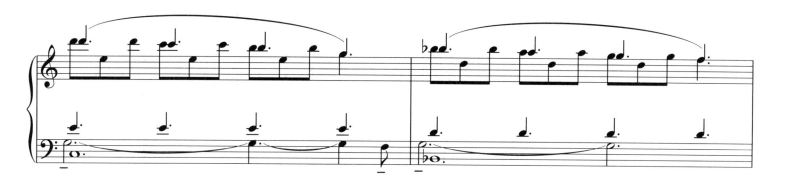

come prima

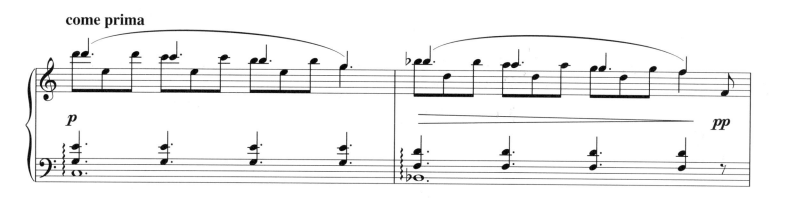

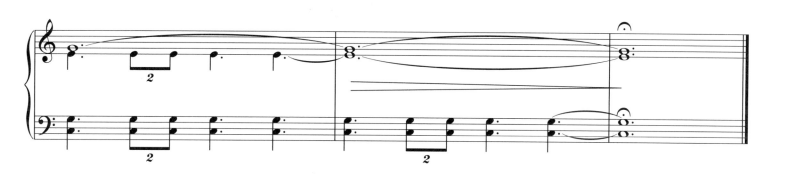

piano concerto no.1
in E minor (romance: larghetto)

By Frederick Chopin

Larghetto (= 68)

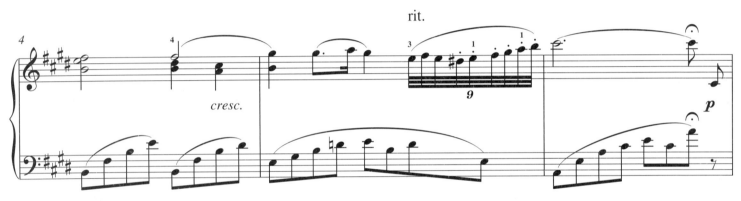

a tempo

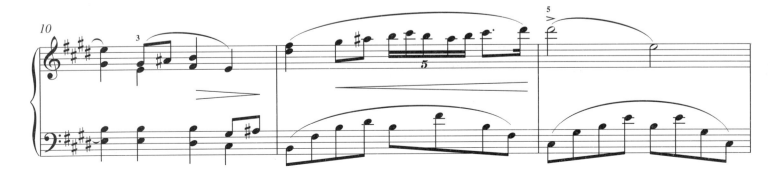

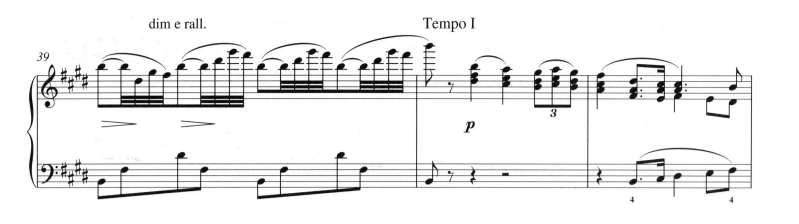

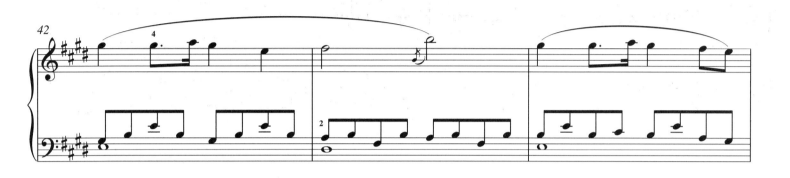

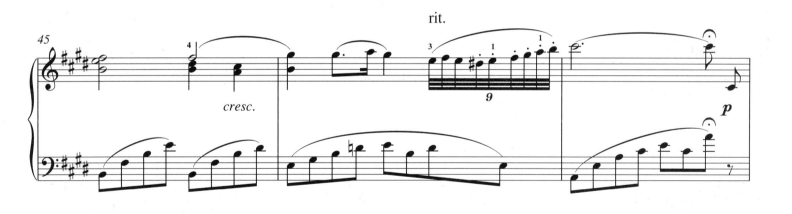

piano concerto no.5
in F minor (2nd movement: largo)

By Johann Sebastian Bach

sarabande
in D minor

By George Frideric Handel

Lento (♩ = 62)

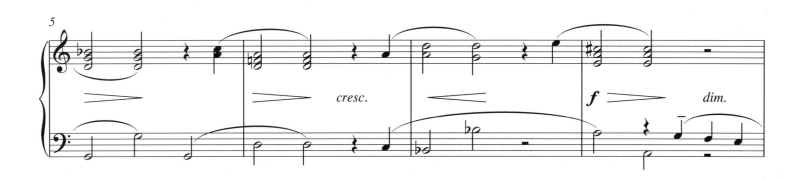

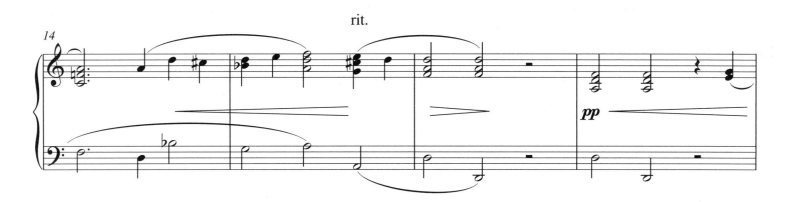

a tempo

molto rit.

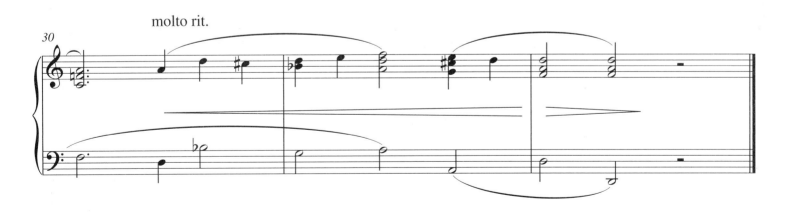

sur le fil
(from *amelie*)

By Yann Tiersen

Rubato ♩ = 92

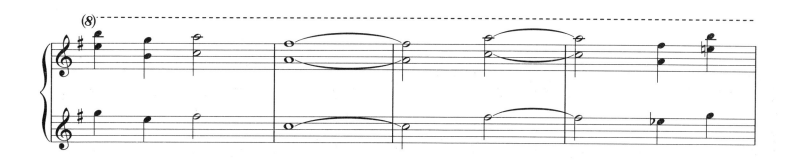

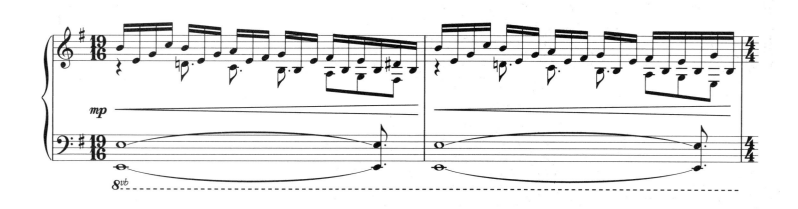

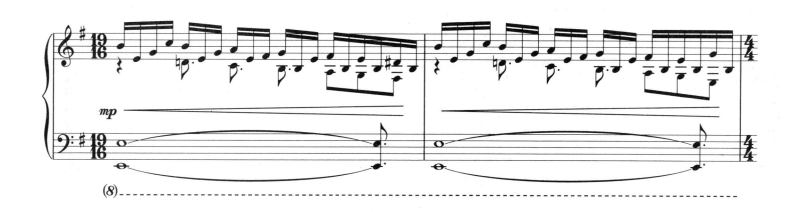

theme
from *inspector morse*

By Barrington Pheloung

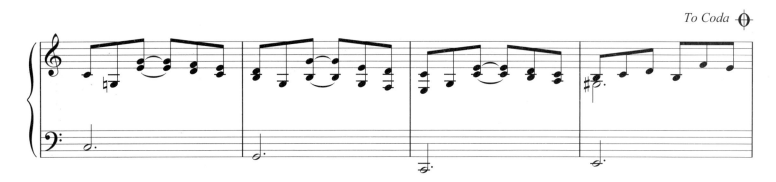

D. 𝄋 al Coda

⊕ CODA

molto rall.